6

7

8

9

10

For my mum, who baked lovely cakes for us every Saturday - C.F.

To M and D with love - J.M.

Published by Brimax,
A division of Autumn Publishing Limited
©2002 Autumn Publishing Limited
Appledram Barns, Chichester PO20 7EQ
Illustrations © Jane Massey 2002

A CIP catalogue record for this book is available
from the British Library.

ISBN 1 85854 461 0 (hardback)
ISBN 1 85854 698 2 (paperback)

Printed in China

The Yummy, Yummy Cake Trick

Written by Colin Fletcher

Illustrated by Jane Massey

BRIMAX

Every Saturday, Harry's mother made cakes – yummy, yummy cakes.

Harry loved cakes.
So did Laura, his big sister.
He could have eaten ten at once!
So could she!

Sometimes there were some broken
ones and his mother would say,
"You two can have these if you like.
But don't forget to share. Be fair."

"Would you like one gingerbread man or two?"
Laura asked sweetly.

"Two! Two, please!" Harry yelled.

"Okay, two for you and one for me! That's fair."
Laura gave Harry two small, broken bits and kept a nearly perfect gingerbread man for herself.

She was always tricking him.
He hated it when she tricked him!

The next Saturday, his mother
made fairy cakes –
yummy, yummy fairy cakes.

"Would you like three fairy cakes or four?" Laura asked him nicely.

"Four! I'll have four, please!"
Harry shouted.

"Okay. Four for you and three for me! That's fair."
She had tricked him again! Harry was so angry.
But she wouldn't trick him next time.

Next time he'd know
what to say!

The next Saturday,
Harry's mother baked jam tarts –
yummy, yummy jam tarts.

And, when Laura said,
"Five tarts or six, Harry?"

He said, "Five. Just five, please."

"Okay, five for you and six for me! That's fair!" said Laura, handing him a plate with five, tiny pieces.

Oh no, poor old Harry. How did that happen?
So Harry decided that *he* would play a trick on *her!*

The next week, his mother made
chocolate chip cookies –
yummy, yummy chocolate chip cookies.

Now. . . let me see, Harry thought.

He very carefully put seven **HUGE**
cookies on one plate. . .
and eight tiny ones on another.

Then he asked her, very politely,
"How many cookies would you like, Laura?"

Laura thought very hard. . .
and then she yelled. . .

"FIFTEEN!" and grabbed them all!
"THAT'S NOT FAIR!" Harry sobbed.
He was just hopeless at tricks.
He always got it wrong.

But Harry's mother had been listening and watching all the time. And *she* had a trick of her own!

"Who's going to bed at 9 o'clock and who's going to bed at 10 o'clock?" she asked them.

"ME AT 10! HARRY AT 9! THAT'S FAIR!"
Laura shouted before Harry had a chance.

"Okay, then!"
Harry's mother said.

"It's 10 o'clock now.
10 o'clock in the morning!
So off to bed with you, young lady!"

"He can help me eat this cake — this yummy, yummy cake!"

1

How many yummy, yummy cakes can you count?

2

3

4

5